Phantasmagoria
33 Songs, Story-lines and Sound Adventures

by Kaye Umansky

with illustrations by Chris Smedley
and sound exploration ideas by Andy Jackson

A & C Black · London

The Magic Canoe

Songs of myth and legend in a mystical soundscape

Introduction

A canoe takes us on a journey through a phantasmagoria of mythical creatures and legends. The songs which describe them are linked by the river, whose waterfalls, rapids and marshy fens are depicted in sound.

Using the material

The songs can be used on their own, perhaps for a classroom project on myth and legend. The ideas for link music can also be used separately in class. Groups of children can make up their own river maps (without songs) and decide how to 'play' them. You might like to introduce them to Smetana's descriptive piece, *Vlatava* (The Moldau) from *Ma Vlast*. This orchestral work describes the journey of a river from its source as a tiny stream in the mountains to the huge broad waterway which flows into the sea, passing forests, villages and cities on the way. Listen to the way the instruments are used to suggest the movement of the river in all its different moods.

For a full performance you need:

Instrumental group one – song accompaniments
Instrumental group two – link music
Singers
Score – the map of the river's course
A small model canoe attached to a long stick
A conductor

The score forms the backdrop to the performance area, so it can be as large as you want to make it. The central feature (see pages 4–5) is a river running from left to right. The mythical creatures and people can be made to stand out from the score by drawing them separately, cutting them out and sandwiching a block of polystyrene or an empty cereal box between the cutout and the score.

After the first song, *Magic canoe*, the person holding the canoe stick begins to move the canoe very slowly along the river. This is the signal for the link music to begin. When the canoe arrives at the Thunderbird, the song *Thunderbird* is performed. The canoe continues its journey to the accompaniment of more link music, stopping each time it comes to a mythical creature. The conductor is really only needed to ensure that the alternating instrumental groups know when to begin and end. You may decide to dovetail the link music with the song accompaniments to make a smoother transition.

Link music

The features of the map are related to the subjects of the songs and both may give the children ideas for devising descriptive sounds for the links. Here are some possibilities:

Mountain crags *(Thunderbird)* – massive chord-clusters on piano, jagged notes on strings, a thunderboard (a large sheet of metal suspended by ropes; a metal dustbin is a good alternative) struck with soft beaters.

Waterfall *(Unicorn)* – muted drum roll on thunderboard or bass drum, a spray of tinkling sounds on soprano glockenspiel, Indian bells, etc.

Dark, evergreen forests *(Bigfoot)* – sustained notes on strings and woodwind, sighing brush strokes on cymbal with wire brush, odd patterings and taps of fingers on a drum skin.

Marshy fens where the river breaks into a maze of meandering streams *(Griffin)* – numerous, interweaving melody lines played on instruments with widely contrasted pitches, and at different dynamic levels.

Deep, still lake *(Excalibur)* – intermittent sounds with long silences between, e.g. metal objects (bells, pipes, triangle) struck with wood and lowered into a bucket of water, deep flute-like notes blown over the tops of large plastic bottles.

Rapids *(The dragons are awake)* – shakers, crackling plastic eggboxes, cymbal clashes.

Whirlpool *(Siren song)* – glass harmonica (run wet fingers round the rims of wine glasses), undulating runs on wind instruments, glissandi on piano.

Broad river estuary *(Songs of dragons and kings)* – oscillating pairs of notes on piano, strings, pitched percussion, sustained notes on bottles, plucked bass notes on guitar.

Programme notes

You can provide your audience with programmes using the notes given with each song, or you might like to begin the performance with a spoken introduction explaining the score, and a little about the subjects of the songs.

Mime and dance

The suggestions for a full performance put the emphasis on sound rather than action. However, opportunities for mime and dance might be explored in class, or possibly in an abridged performance using just the link music, or just the songs.

Classroom activities

Ideas for further sound exploration, games and activities are included with the songs.

THUNDERBIRD

BIGFOOT

UNICORN

GRIFFIN

EXCALIBUR

SIREN SONG

SONGS OF DRAGONS AND KINGS

THE DRAGONS ARE AWAKE

5

Magic canoe

Drifting down river in my red and yellow canoe,
Pull, dip, paddle and swing,
Drifting down river in my red and yellow canoe,
Pull, dip, paddle and swing,
Through a mystical land, where all of my dreams will come true,
Pull, dip, paddle and swing.

Drifting down river where the flowers grow wild in the grass,
Pull, dip, paddle and swing,
Drifting down river where the flowers grow wild in the grass,
Pull, dip, paddle and swing,
All the people are smiling and waving their hands as I pass,
Pull, dip, paddle and swing.

   As past forests and mountains I glide,
   Can't help but wonder what secrets they hide,
   But my canoe has to run with the tide,
   So they go sliding by me.

Drifting down river I'm the king of all I survey,
Pull, dip, paddle and swing,
Drifting down river I'm the king of all I survey,
Pull, dip, paddle and swing,
So farewell, my friends, might see you again one fine day,
Pull, dip, paddle and swing.

GROUP 1 Drif-ting down ri-ver in my red and yel-low ca-

Dreamily

- noe, GROUP 2 *Pull,* *dip,* *pad-dle and* *swing,*

G.1. Drif-ting down ri-ver in my red and yel-low ca-

- noe, G.2 *Pull,* *dip,* *pad-dle and* *swing,* G.1 Through a

my-sti-cal land, where all of my dreams will come true, Pull, dip,

G.2

pad-dle and swing. ALL As past for-ests and moun-tains I glide,

Can't help but won-der what se-crets they hide, But my ca-noe has to

run with the tide, So they go sli - ding by me.

D.C. al Fine

Singing the song

Divide into two groups. The second group sings the refrain, *Pull, dip, paddle and swing.*

Song accompaniment

Think of a sound effect for the splashing of the canoe paddle, e.g. tap the rim of a tambourine on the first beat of alternate bars.

Chime bars or bass xylophone can play the refrain:

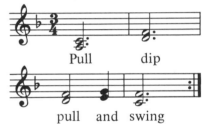

Pull dip

pull and swing

Indian bells

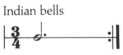

Use the first eight bars as an introduction.

7

Thunderbird

Big bird, flying high,
Thunderbird, Thunderbird,
Dark clouds fill the sky,
Thunderbird.

Big bird, hear him call,
Thunderbird, Thunderbird,
Rain begins to fall,
Thunderbird.

Big bird blinks his eye,
Thunderbird, Thunderbird,
Fiery arrows fly,
Thunderbird.

Big bird passes on,
Thunderbird, Thunderbird,
Now the storm has gone,
Thunderbird.

North American Indian tribes likened thunder to the flapping wings of the Thunderbird. The Thunderbird looked like an enormous eagle and as it flew high above the earth, the whole sky would darken. On its back it carried a huge lake of water, which would spill over, causing the rain to fall. Lightning was caused by the blinking of the great bird's eye.

Singing the song
Begin very softly and increase the volume through to the end of the third verse, then drop down through the last verse to a whisper in the last line.

Song accompaniment
Devise sound effects to give an impression of dark clouds, the Thunderbird's call, the rain, fiery arrows. Try dropping rice onto a tin tray, making shakers with different fillings, clashing cymbals, a low-pitched ominous drone on cello, and so on. Increase the volume from one verse to the next and use a thunderboard (see page 3) at the climax of the song.

Tambour and soft stick

There are many legends about what causes thunder – make up one of your own.

Thunderbird knitting score (instrumental)

Transfer the score onto a large sheet of paper and colour in the squares according to the key. The score is read from left to right, column by column. Each column has a second's duration – the seconds are numbered at the bottom of the score. It will help to choose a conductor to call out the numbers. The colours refer to instruments, and the piece is much louder in the middle because of the number of instruments playing there and because of the greater density of colour. (Introduce the terms *crescendo* and *decrescendo*.)

Playing the piece (two approaches)

If you use one instrument per colour, the players will need to work out beforehand where they need to crescendo and decrescendo in response to the density of colour, e.g. the drum needs to crescendo through 11–15, and decrescendo through 15–19.

Alternatively, you can roughly match quantities of instruments to colour density, and divide them between groups of players, e.g. one group to play the head, two groups for the body, and a fourth for the feet. Group 1 might play 2 suspended cymbals, 4 rattles and piano. Group 2 – 1 woodblock, 1 thunderboard, 1 rattle, 1 drum. Group 3 – 2 drums, 2 thunderboards, 2 rattles. Group 4 – 2 suspended cymbals.

Key:

- **Br** — Wood block (brown)
- **R** — Thunderboard (red)
- **Bl** — Large drum (black)
- **W** — Rattles (white)
- **Y** — Suspended cymbals (yellow)
- **G** — Chord cluster on piano (green) (hold down pedal)

GROUP 1 · GROUP 2 · GROUP 3 · GROUP 4

1 2 3 4 5 6 7 8 9 10 11 12 13 14 15 16 17 18 19 20 21 22 23 24 25 26 27 28 29 30 31 32 33 34 35

Unicorn

Unicorn, oh where were you born?
  Underneath a waterfall
  On a misty mountain tall,
  Where the eagles swoop and call,
  That's where I was born.

Unicorn, oh what is your horn?
  Shiny as a silver spoon,
  It can play a fairy tune,
  Make you wish you had the moon,
  That, child, is my horn.

Unicorn, don't leave me forlorn,
  Slowly he began to fade,
  Vanished from the woodland glade,
  Gone to find a fair young maid,
  Leaving me to mourn.

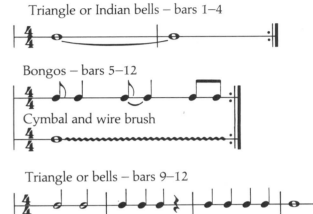

ea - gles swoop and call,___ That's where I was born.

Bb/G C7/A7 Dm/Bm Gm/Em F/D C7/A7 F/D

Song accompaniment

The last four bars can be used as an introduction.

Triangle or Indian bells – bars 1–4

Bongos – bars 5–12

Cymbal and wire brush

Triangle or bells – bars 9–12

Glockenspiel or xylophone – play the bass line of the piano accompaniment.

The legendary unicorn was a creature rather like a horse. It was said to be pure white with a small, goat-like beard, the tail of a lion and a single, long, spiralled horn growing from its forehead. It was able to run at great speed, and the legends tell that only a young, unmarried girl could tame it. If she sat all alone in a wood (and luck was on her side), a unicorn would appear and lay its head in her lap.

A unicorn's horn was said to have magical powers, for if it was dipped into a dirty pool or stream, the water would immediately become clean again. It was also thought that a wine cup made from the horn would change colour and warn the drinker if the wine was poisoned.

Design an anti-pollution poster using a unicorn emblem. Choose an aspect such as acid rain, or river pollution.

11

Bigfoot country

Through the forest, by the river,
  Bigfoot country,
Ten sharp arrows in my quiver,
  Bigfoot country,
Always doomed to be behind him,
Wonder if I'll ever find him?
  Bigfoot, Bigfoot, Bigfoot country.

To the mountains I'll be going,
  Bigfoot country,
Always cold, forever snowing,
  Bigfoot country,
Sometimes running, sometimes walking,
Never resting, always stalking,
  Bigfoot, Bigfoot, Bigfoot country.

Does he watch me, does he fear me?
  Bigfoot country,
Even now could he be near me?
  Bigfoot country,
Could he be a fabrication,
Product of imagination?
  Bigfoot, Bigfoot, Bigfoot country.

Giant footsteps I am trailing,
  Bigfoot country,
Does he know my strength is failing?
  Bigfoot country,
Farewell, friend, for night is falling,
Far away I hear him calling,
  Bigfoot, Bigfoot, Bigfoot country.

In the deep forests of the mountain country of North America, huge footprints have been sighted. These footprints have given rise to the legend of Bigfoot — a huge, shaggy, ape-like creature, much taller than a human being. The Indian name for this giant is Sasquatch.

Bigfoot is said to walk upright, and at night its wild howling echoes through the mountains. Some people claim to have glimpsed Bigfoot, and it is possible that there are more than one living amongst the high peaks, but no one has ever succeeded in capturing one, and no skeleton has ever been discovered.

Al - ways doomed to be be-hind him, Won-der if I'll e - ver find him?

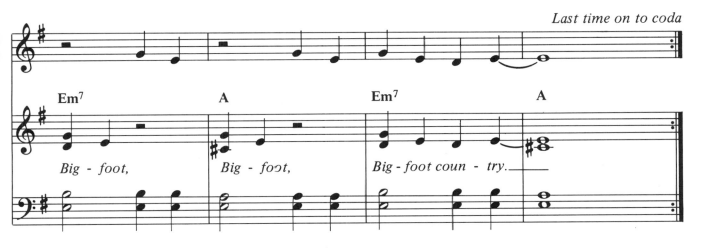

Last time on to coda

Big - foot, Big - foot, Big - foot coun - try.

Coda: repeat ad lib, gradually fading

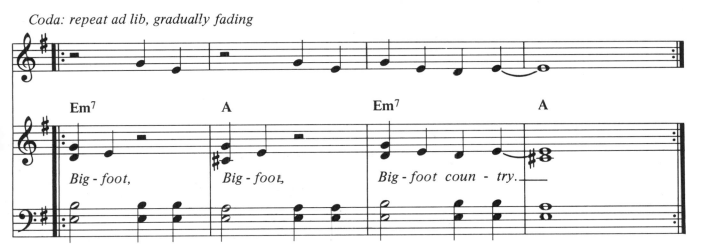

Big - foot, Big - foot, Big - foot coun - try.

Song accompaniment

Use the coda as an introduction and interlude between verses. A soloist might sing the first, third, fifth and sixth lines, with a chorus singing softly the *Bigfoot country* refrain.

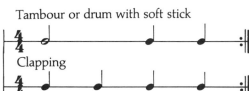

Tambour or drum with soft stick

Clapping

Practise fading out the percussion and clapping during the coda.

Make up a stalking dance to go with the song. Involve creeping, climbing, listening, crawling and running movements.

Explorers (game)

This is a game for improving listening skills. Divide into a larger and a smaller group. The larger group spreads out around the room and each person pretends to be part of a huge forest: a tree or an animal, perhaps a stream. Each person thinks of a very faint sound to represent what they have chosen to be; a mouse might make a squeaking sound and a tree might sigh as it sways in the wind. The smaller group are the explorers, who are blindfolded. They have to make their way through the forest by listening out for and avoiding the obstacles in their path. If they bump into each other, they whisper the password, 'Bigfoot'.

Development

One of the larger group is chosen to be Bigfoot, and no one makes a sound unless an explorer touches them. If an explorer touches Bigfoot, he roars, and the explorers all retreat to base.

13

Griffin

Griffin is a mixed-up monster,
But doesn't mind a bit,
He's a little bit of this,
A little bit of that,
And nothing ever seems to fit,
He's got this eagle's head with great big ears,
A lion's tail stuck on the rear,
And everybody peers, he looks so queer,
But he doesn't mind a bit.
    Mixed-up, mixed-up, oughta get him fixed up,
    Mixed-up, mixed-up, oughta get him fixed up,
    Mixed-up, mixed-up, oughta get him fixed up,
    Griffin is a mixed-up monster.

Griffin is a mixed-up monster,
Who gives a strange effect,
He's a little bit of this,
A little bit of that,
And a bit of what you don't expect,
He's got these ten sharp nails which grow so long,
Two big wings which look real strong,
And everybody stares 'cos he's all wrong,
And gives a strange effect.
    Mixed-up, mixed-up, oughta get him fixed up . . .

Chant (repeat chorus quietly as background to chant)
'Hey, Mr Griffin, you're a mixed-up mess!'
'Well, that's okay, I couldn't care less.'
'Aren't you ashamed to look the way you do?'
'If I look weird, well, how about you?'

Coda (fade)
Mixed-up, mixed-up, oughta get him fixed up . . .

14

The griffin (or gryphon) is one of the strangest fabulous animals. It had the head of an eagle with two huge ears. It had the body, hind legs and tail of a lion, and great bird wings, which never closed, were attached to its back. It was said to build its nest high in the mountains, lining it with gold, which was stolen or pecked from the rocks with its fearsome beak. The writer, Lewis Carroll, put a griffin into his famous book *Alice's Adventures in Wonderland*. The beast was often portrayed on shields and banners in medieval times.

Singing the song

Divide into three groups — one for the chorus, and the second and third for the dialogue in the chant. Everyone sings together in the verse.

Song accompaniment

Use the last four bars as an introduction.

Griffin consequences (instrumental)

First of all, the children need to make their own score by playing the game of consequences. Divide a long sheet of paper into sections with vertical black lines. Next fold the paper backwards and forwards along the lines like a fan so that only one section can be seen at a time. On the first section, someone draws the griffin's nose. Turn the paper over to the next section and draw the face, then the neck (you might take several sections for this), and so on until the griffin is complete. (Make sure you have a head, neck, front body, wings and forelegs, rear and hind legs, and a tail.) The result might look something like this:

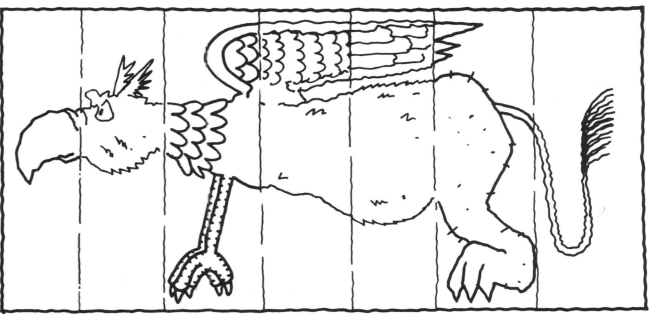

groups — one to each of the following notes — and learn to recognise which colour refers to your group:

A – red   B – blue   D – brown
E – yellow   G – green

Fix the score on a wall where everyone can see it and choose a conductor to point to the various sections. The conductor may point from left to right, or right to left, or move freely between sections. When a section is indicated, the group whose colour is represented plays its note. If there are several colours, then several groups play at the same time. If the conductor moves quickly between the sections

Now colour the griffin using only red, blue, green, yellow and brown. Allow the colours to overlap the sections, even having several colours in one.

Everybody chooses an instrument which can play a definite pitch — xylophone, chime bar, piano, electronic keyboard, recorder, guitar, etc. Divide into six

of the griffin, the effect is of a constantly changing and varied pattern of sound, symbolising the griffin.

Younger children might start off with a simpler version — one colour and one note to each of five sections. Divide into groups of five, and try playing each other's griffins.

Excalibur

Come, Merlin, my wizard,
We'll ride to the lake
Where no birds sing,
I'm frightened to go
But the risk I will take
To bring back a sword for a king.
    A mighty sword,
    A wonderful sword
    Waits to be claimed
    By its rightful lord,
    Excalibur! Excalibur!
    The sword for a king.

The waters they parted,
The earth it did shake,
The birds took wing.
The hand of a lady
Rose up from the lake,
Holding a sword for a king.
    A mighty sword...

I rode back to Camelot,
Sword in my hand,
The bells did ring.
Tonight will be dancing
And joy in the land
For mine is the sword for a king.
    A mighty sword...

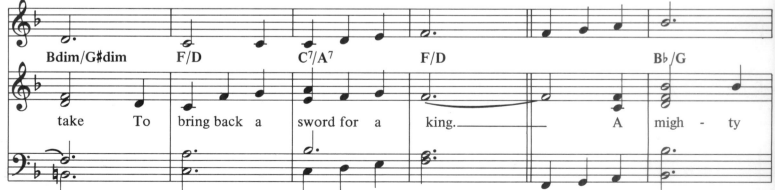

16

Bb/G Am/F#m Dm/Bm G7/E7

sword, A won-der-ful sword Waits to be claimed By its

C7/A7 F/D Bb/G F/D

right-ful lord, Ex-ca-li-bur! Ex-ca-li-

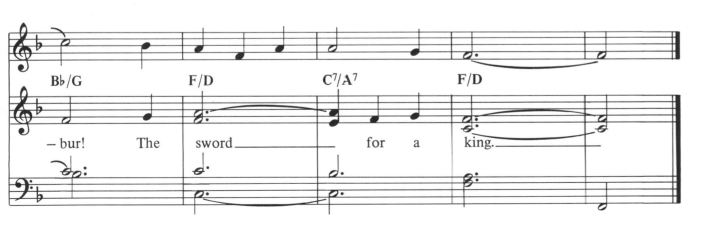

Bb/G F/D C7/A7 F/D

-bur! The sword for a king.

Many stories have been told about the days of knighthood. One of the best-known legends is that of King Arthur and the Knights of the Round Table. According to the legend, Arthur's knights were the bravest, truest, and boldest knights of all time.

Arthur was brought up by the great magician Merlin. He proved his right to be king by pulling a sword from a stone, but his most famous sword was called Excalibur. This sword was a gift from the Lady of the Lake. The tale goes that an arm rose out of the water holding Excalibur. Merlin rowed King Arthur out to accept it. When Arthur was dying, he ordered one of his knights to cast the sword back into the lake. A hand rose from the water, caught Excalibur, and vanished.

Song accompaniment
Use the last eight bars of the chorus (with the up beat) as an introduction.

Tambour – chorus

Tuned percussion – play the bass line of the piano accompaniment.

The dragons are awake

There's the sound of thunder
And it's coming from down under,
Run! Run! The dragons are awake!

There's the smell of ashes
And a great tail lashes,
Run! Run! The dragons are awake!

Now the mountain's quivering,
The earth is shivering,
Run! Run! The dragons are awake.

There's a roaring and a screaming
And a red eye gleaming,
Run! Run! The dragons are awake!

Now in flight they fill the skies,
There's a sight to terrorize.

There's a honking and a hooting
And the flames come shooting,
Run! Run! The dragons are awake!

Run very fast
Or this day will be your last,
Run! Run! The dragons are awake!

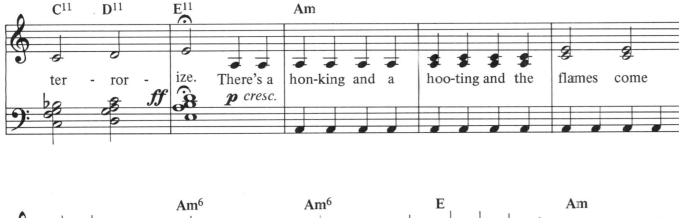

Dragons have long been a part of folklore. They are usually depicted as huge, scaly reptiles with wings. Their homes were generally caves in the mountains, where they lay on piles of stolen treasure. Some were able to breathe fire, which made them formidable enemies. Sometimes, sacrifices were offered to dragons in order to stop them destroying everything in sight. There are many stories of young princesses being rescued from this terrible fate by brave warriors or knights.

Not all dragons are quite so fearsome. Chinese dragons are very different from the ferocious European breed. They are depicted as colourful, snake-like, friendly creatures with the ability to appear in human form.

Song accompaniment

Use the deepest drum or tambour you have for a menacing roll, errupting into two huge cymbal clashes on 'Run! Run!' To add to the menace of the crescendo, bring in more instruments which shake and rumble — tambourines, maracas, a wobble board. For contrast use triangles and bells in the short bridge section. The bass line of the piano part could be echoed on bass xylophone or chime bars:

Dragon hunt — if you look for dragons, you will spot them everywhere — on inn signs, badges, pottery, etc. Make a list.

19

Siren song

Can you hear us singing, sailor boy, sailor boy?
Can you hear us singing, sailor boy?
Though the winds blow strong can you hear our song?
Can you hear us singing, sailor boy?
    Oh Jack, beware the Siren song,
    Though temptation's very strong.
    Hide your ears to block the sound
    Or the ship will go aground.

Can you hear us calling, sailor boy, sailor boy?
Can you hear us calling, sailor boy?
Though the waves are tall can you hear our call?
Can you hear us calling, sailor boy?
    Oh Jack, beware the Siren song . . .

Can you hear us crying, sailor boy, sailor boy?
Can you hear us crying, sailor boy?
Though the seas rise high, can you hear our cry?
Can you hear us crying, sailor boy?
    Oh Jack, beware the Siren song,
    Though temptation's very strong,
    Hide your ears to block the sound
    Or the ship will go aground.
    Turn your back and then for sure
    You will see your home once more.

Last time to coda

C ... **G** **Em** **A⁷** **D** **G**

Hide your ears to | block the sound Or the | ship will go a - | ground.

Coda

A⁷ **D** **G** **C**

ship will go a - | ground. | Turn your back and

G **Em** **A⁷** **D** **G**

then for sure You will | see your home once | more.

The legend of the Sirens originated in ancient Greece. The hero Odysseus met with them on a voyage which took him to the islands lying between Italy and Sicily. The Sirens were creatures that had the upper body of a woman and the lower body of a bird. They were said to lure sailors to their death by singing in voices of incredible, haunting beauty. Odysseus wanted to hear their songs, but knew that if he did he was doomed. But he thought of a plan, and ordered his crew to stuff up their ears with wax. He made them tie him to the mast so that he could hear the Sirens without being able to go to them. So it was that Odysseus heard the song of the Sirens and lived to tell the tale.

Singing the song

Divide into two groups, one to be Sirens, the other to be sailors.

Song accompaniment

Use a glass harmonica (see page 3) to give an unearthly quality to the Sirens' part of the song. The glasses can be tuned to G, C and D by adding water – play the bass line of the piano accompaniment, transposed to the range of the glasses. Chime bars can also play the chords of the piano accompaniment. Wave a strip of paper over the sound holes to give a shimmering effect. Run soft beaters over the bars of a glockenspiel.

In contrast, use clear, bold sounds in the second half of the song – a xylophone playing the bass line, a drum beating a regular rhythm for the oars.

Songs of dragons and kings

Oh where are you going, tall knight in shining armour?
  Sing a song of dragons and kings,
Oh please may I go with you, though I'm just a simple farmer?
  Sing a song of dragons and kings,
I've never seen a dragon, and I hear you've come to fight,
  Sing a song of dragons and kings,
I'm longing for adventure, may I ride with you, Sir Knight?
  Sing a song of dragons and kings.

And we'll ride together through wild and windy weather,
  No matter what tomorrow brings,
Where you lead I'll follow, through cavern, cave and hollow,
  Singing songs of dragons, songs of dragons,
  Songs of dragons and kings.

Oh think again, young farmer, the knight did softly say,
  Sing a song of dragons and kings,
I fought my final dragon one year ago today.
  Sing a song of dragons and kings.
In that cave I lay a-dying, yet I made the final kill,
  Sing a song of dragons and kings,
In a grave my body's lying, yet my spirit wanders still,
  Sing a song of dragons and kings.

And we'll ride together . . .

They called him Dragonslayer. He sat tall in the saddle of his white mare, silver armour gleaming in the moonlight. This was Tom's chance. All his life he had longed for adventure. Shouldering his pitchfork, he boldly stepped forward and spoke to the pale, still figure.

'Sir, forgive my boldness – but are you not the famous knight they call Dragonslayer? He who has spilled the blood of a hundred dragons?'

'Aye, lad. So they call me,' came the quiet voice from behind the closed vizor.

'Then, sir – hear my request. I wish to be your page, sir. I'll ride at your side, tend your horse, polish your sword – anything if I may come with you. I don't want to be a farmer, you see. I want to fight dragons!'

The knight sighed. 'What is your name, boy?'

'Tom, sir.'

'Well, Tom. So you would turn your back on home and family to ride with me eh?'

'Gladly!'

'And nothing will make you change your mind?'

'Nothing.'

'Even this?'

The knight slowly raised one arm. The moon went behind a cloud as he lifted his vizor – but not before Tom caught a glimpse of the sight which would haunt his dreams forever.

The vizor was empty. The knight had no face.

Singing the song

Divide into three groups (or two soloists and chorus), the third group singing the refrain, *Sing a song of dragons and kings,* and the first two taking the parts of the farmer and the knight.

FLIGHT OF THE STARSHIP SILVER GREY

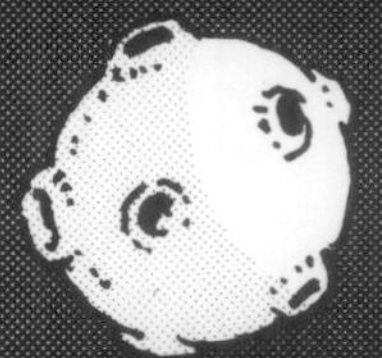

A musical space drama

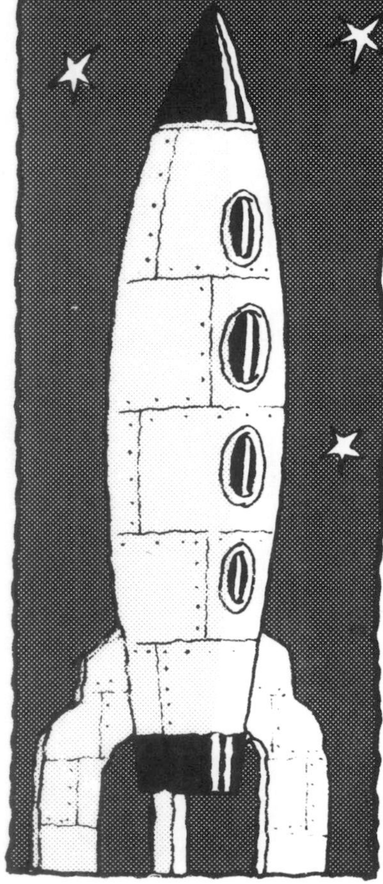

Cast (in order of appearance)

The Earthling

The Star Captain

The crew

The Professor

The robot salesman (X4423)

Robot Number Nine

The other robots

The Gobbledegook

Introduction

Like all the others in this book, the songs in this section are intended to stand on their own as part of a class music lesson. However, sung together they can form the basis of a musical space drama, to be performed in assembly, or as a full-blown end of term production before an invited audience. You may prefer to improvise your own plot. However, a story-line has been developed (with sample dialogue and staging suggestions) to give you an idea of the sort of thing that can be done.

The story

A child (the Earthling) is taken on board the Starship Silver Grey, which is touring the universe. His/her adventures include experiencing zero gravity; landing on the Planet Roboticus and choosing a robot to join the crew; making friends with an alien; being examined by the ship's Professor, the inventor of X-ray spectacles; travelling through deep space, and operating a time machine. The play ends with the child waking up safely in bed, wondering whether or not the whole adventure has been a dream, but determined to travel into space again.

The scenes are linked by extracts from the captain's log and, of course, the songs, which are sung by the Space Singers. A group of instrumentalists perform the accompaniments and sound effects.

Staging

The action takes place in three main areas. A fourth is required for the Space Singers and instrumentalists. How you decide to do this depends on the design and lay-out of your hall. If your hall already has a stage, you may wish to use this for the entire production, changing backdrops between scenes. Alternatively, you could build four smaller stages using rostra blocks. The areas are as follows:

The Earthling's bedroom – at its simplest, this merely needs to include a bed and a window with partially drawn curtains, looking out on the night sky. You can, of course, embellish as much as you wish.

Interior of Starship Silver Grey – most of the action takes place here, so the set should be fairly large. The Professor's laboratory can be a smaller area set to one side, indicating that it is a separate room. If a backdrop is used, it could portray banks of technical equipment, portholes looking out into space, etc.

The Planet Roboticus – if a backdrop is used, it should portray an alien environment. Exactly what form this should take can be discussed with the children, e.g. a purple sky with two moons, strange vegetation, etc.

The Space Singers – the Space Singers are a group of children who sing throughout the production. In some cases, the actors join in with the songs, but the Space Singers provide the musical bedrock of the production, together with the instrumentalists.

Sound effects

Sound effects are required at various points during the play. These include the noise of the starship landing and taking off, the humming of the time machine, etc. The selection of instruments used and the effects themselves should be discussed with the children.

Costumes

It really is up to you how much time and trouble you wish to take. The costumes can be extremely elaborate, or very simple. Discuss with the children their ideas of how the captain and crew of an alien starship might look. Large cardboard boxes and tin foil can form the basis of the robots' costumes. As for the Gobbledegook, the sky's the limit! Wonders can be achieved with the use of a mask and/or various extra attached limbs or tentacles.

Props

The only props that need to be specifically made are the X-ray spectacles, the time machine and the rocket. The Space Singers can each have a pair of odd-looking specs to wear when they sing the song. Each child could make their own pair – the more weird and wonderful the better. The Professor's pair should be the strangest of the lot.

The time machine can either be a cardboard cutout with a door that opens, and windows, or something that the Earthling can actually sit in, with various strange antennae stuck on. The children might like to design one. It can either be present in the earlier scene set in the lab, or can be brought on later. It depends how flimsy the design is. At the end of the drama, a large rocket ship has to be constructed on stage. This can consist in the main of separate, painted cardboard boxes devised so that they can be rapidly assembled on stage into the finished rocket.

Lighting

Although some stunning effects can be achieved by theatrical lighting (e.g. being suddenly plunged into darkness when the Earthling is beamed up), it isn't strictly necessary. With the use of screens and a bit of imagination, the play can be performed quite easily without it. However, the following scenario assumes that lights will be available.

The Starship Silver Grey

(Dim light comes up on an Earthling's bedroom. He/she is asleep in bed. Distant rumbling is heard. As the Star Captain's disembodied voice speaks, flashing lights are seen through the bedroom window. The Earthling wakes, rubs his/her eyes, goes to the window and looks out in wonderment.)

Captain's voice (over PA system): 'Star Captain's log entry, first day of the first month, year two thousand and eighty eight. The Starship Silver Grey continues her fact-finding tour of the universe. We are now approaching a small, little-known solar system, consisting of a star with nine planets circling around it. The Professor has been doing some research, and tells me that only one of these planets, named Earth, is likely to contain intelligent life forms. Our intention is to seek out an Earthling, should such a thing exist, and bring it on board the Silver Grey for further study. The crew is preparing to land. End of entry.' (The rumbling grows in volume.)

Earthling: Mum? Dad? Quick, come and see the lights! Something's happening in the sky... it's a huge ship, it's coming down to land... it's blotting out the stars...

(The rumbling reaches a crescendo, there is an intense flash of light, and we are plunged into darkness.)

Earthling (faintly): Mum! What's happening? Where are you? I'm being sucked up... help!

I'm the Captain of this starship,
Would you like to step inside?
I've travelled far beyond the Milky Way,
Gonna beam you up and take you
On a trillion light year ride,
So welcome to the Starship Silver Grey.
  Stand by, space crew, to your place, crew,
  Engines roaring, sparks are soaring,
  Rockets firing, check that wiring!
  Stand by, crew, all systems go!

I'm the Captain of this starship,
Would you like to join my crew?
I hope I can persuade you all to stay,
And we'll roam the stars together
On our trillion light year ride
In the safety of the Starship Silver Grey.
  Stand by, space crew, to your place, crew,
  Engines roaring, sparks are soaring,
  Rockets firing, check that wiring!
  Stand by crew, all systems go!

Five – four – three – two – one – BLAST OFF!

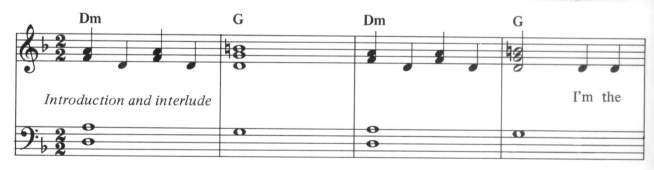

tra - velled far be - | yond the Mil-ky | Way, _____ | | Gon-na | beam you up and | take you On a

tril-lion light year | ride, | So | wel-come to the | Star-ship Sil-ver | Grey. _____ |

Chorus

Stand by, space crew, | to your place, crew, | En-gines roa - ring, | sparks are soa-ring, | Ro-ckets fi-ring, *Crescendo* | check that wi-ring!

Stand by, crew, all | sys-tems go! *ff* | *ff* (chant) Five - four - | three - two | - one | *glissando (black notes)* | BLAST OFF!

(During the song, the lights come up slowly on the set of the Starship's interior. The Captain and crew are frozen, caught in mid action, until the final crashing chord, when they come alive. Some are seated before computers, some are filling in astrological wall charts, etc. The Captain is standing with his back to the audience, gazing through a porthole into space. He turns and smiles kindly as the Earthling, pyjama-clad and rubbing his/her eyes, enters. The crew stare curiously.)

Gravity Zero

Captain: Welcome! Welcome aboard, Earthling. (*He bows*)

Earthling: Wh -what's happening? Where am I?

Captain: Why, you're on board my starship, of course. The mighty Starship Silver Grey. I am the Star Captain. This is your lucky day, little Earthling. You have been chosen to join us on a ride.

Earthling: A ride? Where to? How far are we going?

Captain: A trillion or so light years.

Earthling: Oh. Not that far, then. Er — you don't happen to have a pair of slippers I could borrow? My feet are freezing.

(*Enter the Professor with a pair of large, silver boots*)

Professor: Aha! At last, an Earthling to study. Odd little creature. What's it asking for?

Captain: Something called slippers, Professor.

Professor: Slippers? Never heard of them. No, these gravity boots are what you need, Earthling. With suction grippers. Shortly we'll be approaching gravity zero. If you don't have your boots on, you'll float off.

Earthling: Really? I like the sound of that. Tell me more.

(*Lights up on the Space Singers. If so desired, the Earthling, Captain and crew can join in the song. It might be fun to develop a gravity mime or dance during the song, involving the Earthling putting on the boots as the Professor and crew dance around him.*)

Fat and stout was Emperor Nero,
He weighed nothing in gravity zero,
Gravity, gravity, what hilarity,
Gravity, gravity zero,
Gravity, gravity zero.

Hercules was a mighty big hero,
He weighed nothing in gravity zero,
Gravity, gravity, what hilarity,
Gravity, gravity zero,
Gravity, gravity zero.

Up we go to the chandelier-o,
We weigh nothing in gravity zero,
Gravity, gravity, what hilarity,
Gravity, gravity zero,
Gravity, gravity zero.

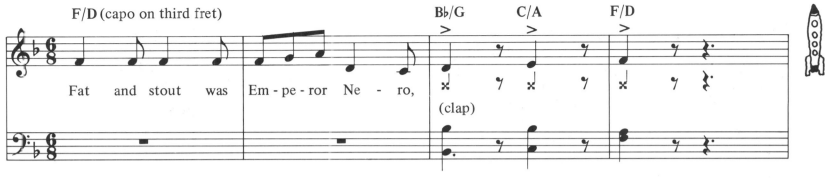

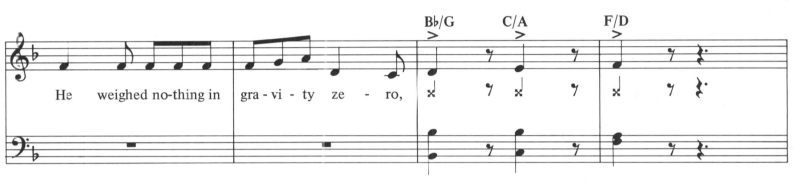

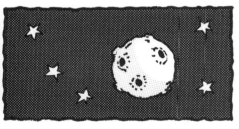

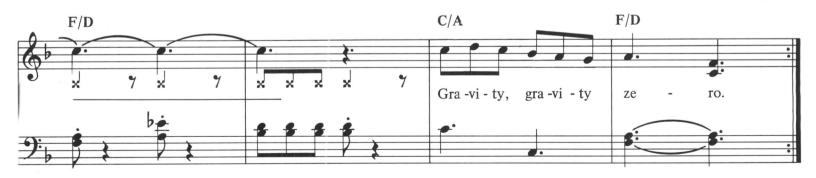

Crew member: Captain, we're approaching the Planet Roboticus.

Captain: Good. We'll stop off and pick up an extra robot. There's usually an end of season sale on round about this time. Attention, crew! Take up your stations and prepare for landing.

Earthling: The Planet Roboticus! Wow! This I can't wait to see.

The Grand Robot Sale

Hands up, e-very-one who'd like to have a ro - bot!
Give a lit-tle twid-dle to the mid-dle of your ro - bot,

Yes, sir! No, sir!
One lump or two, sir?

Tell me where to go, sir.
Now what shall I do, sir?

Su-per-doo-per e-lec-tro-nic au-to-ma-tic ro-bot,

Who, sir? Me, sir?
Yes, sir! No, sir!

Have a cup of tea, sir.

1, 3

2, 4

Three bags full!

Fine

(*Lights up on the Space Singers and the Planet Roboticus. A line of robots file in, led by X4423, the robot sales manager. Robot Number Nine is at the end. X4423 sings the first and third lines of the verses and the bridge. The robots, or Space Singers, sing the other lines, holding their noses. They can invent some jerky, robotic movements*).

Hands up, everyone who'd like to have a robot!
   Yes, sir! No, sir! Tell me where to go, sir.
Superdooper-electronic-automatic robot,
   Who, sir? Me, sir? Have a cup of tea, sir.

Give a little twiddle to the middle of your robot,
   One lump or two, sir? Now what shall I do, sir?
Superdooper-electronic-automatic robot,
   Yes, sir! No, sir! Three bags full!

Buy one, try one, here's a little shy one,
That one's my one, he's for me.
Small and fat with an odd tin hat,
And a five-year guarantee, so

Hands up everyone who'd like to have a robot . . .
(*Repeat through to 'three bags full!'*)

Buy one, try one, here's a lit-tle shy one, That one's my one, he's for me.

Small and fat with an odd tin hat, And a five - year gua-ran-tee, so

D.C. al fine

X4423: Roll up! Roll up for the Grand Robot Sale! Wonderful bargains! Each one comes with its own oil can and a five year guarantee! I've got tall ones, small ones, thin ones, tin ones, tiny ones, shiny ones — each programmed to meet your every need!

(Enter the Star Captain and the Earthling.)

Captain: Good morning, Robot X4423. Any bargains?

X4423: Well! If it isn't the Star Captain. Haven't seen you for a few hundred years, sir. Another tour of the universe, is it?

Captain: Yes, we like to keep our eye on things. Allow me to introduce this Earthling. He's joined us for a little tour.

X4423: Hmm. An Earthling eh? Most peculiar. No offence, of course. Now then, Captain, how can I help you? I've got a fine collection here, at knock-down prices.

Captain: I need one who can do odd jobs. Tea-making, cleaning, that sort of thing.

X4423: No problem sir. No problem at all. They can all do that with their eyes closed. Take your pick.

Captain: What do you think, Earthling? Which one shall we choose?

Earthling: Can we have that little shy one at the end, please?

(Number Nine hops up and down excitedly.)

Captain: Certainly. Put it on my account, would you, X4423?

X4423: With pleasure, Captain. *(To robot)* Right, off you go then, Number Nine. And make sure you oil yourself regularly and don't get into any trouble. Nice meeting you, Earthling.

Earthling: Goodbye, Mr X4423. Come on, Number Nine.

(They follow the Captain off stage.)

X4423 *(staring after them)*: An Earthling, eh? Most peculiar. I wonder if they're all striped like that?

(LIGHTS DOWN)

So what?

(*In darkness, we hear the second extract from the Captain's log.*)

Captain's voice: 'Continuation of Star Captain's log. Number Nine performs its duties satisfactorily, although its tea is a little on the strong side and it always forgets I take two sugars. We are now heading into deep space. The Earthling has settled down well, and appears to be enjoying itself. The Professor has been interrogating it at some length for his report.'

(*Lights up on the Spaceship interior. The crew is busy at work. The Star Captain is writing his log. Number Nine bustles about with cups of tea. The Professor is examining the Earthling. He is measuring his/her head, listening to the chest with a stethoscope, etc, and taking notes. There follows an interruption. A crew member rushes in.*)

Crew member: Captain! Alien stowaway found in the bottom hold, sir.

Captain: Oh no, not again. Another Gobbledegook, I suppose. Why can't they stay on their own planet? All right. Bring it in.

(*The crew member beckons, and the Gobbledegook shuffles in, looking sheepish. It stands before the Captain with head bowed.*)

Captain (*sternly*): I might have known. You Gobbledegooks just can't resist hitching a free ride, can you?

(*The Gobbledegook shakes its head and shuffles ashamedly.*)

Captain: I've a good mind to send you out the ejector hatch into deep space. That would teach you a lesson.

(*The Gobbledegook displays signs of alarm, leaping up and down and gibbering. The Earthling takes pity on it.*)

Earthling: Oh, no! Please don't do that, Captain. I'm sure it's harmless. I'll take care of it and make sure it doesn't get in the way.

Captain: Very well. I'll let you off, just this once.

(*The Gobbledegook throws its tentacles around the Earthling in a display of affection.*)

Captain: I should warn you, Earthling. Gobbledegooks might look ferocious, but they're very friendly. From now on, it'll never leave your side.

Earthling: That's all right. I've always wanted to be friends with an alien.

(*Lights up on the Space Singers.*)

My friend's orange with a long, green nose,
His teeth are yellow and arranged in rows,
He comes from a planet where the blue
  grass grows
But inside he's just like me.
  So what? So what, so what?
  Who cares how many eyes he's got?
  He's my friend and I like him a lot,
  So what? So what?

My friend's orange with a big, bald head,
His feet are furry and his eyes are red,
I can't say his name and so I call him Fred,
And inside he's just like me.
  So what? So what ...

(LIGHTS DOWN)

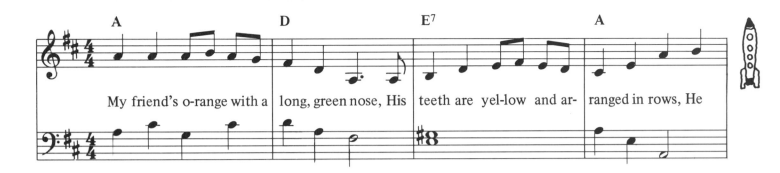

My friend's o-range with a | long, green nose, His | teeth are yel-low and ar- | ranged in rows, He

comes from a pla-net where the | blue grass grows But in- | side he's just like | me. So

what? So | what, so what? | Who cares how ma-ny | eyes he's got?

He's my friend and I | like him a lot, So | what? So | what?

X-ray vision

(*Again, we hear the Captain's voice in the darkness.*)

Captain's voice: 'Continuation of Star Captain's log. The Professor has completed his report on the Earthling, and is now back at work on his X-ray spectacles. He tells me he expects a breakthrough any day.'

(*Lights up on Professor's lab. The Professor is at his workbench, putting the finishing touches to an odd-looking pair of spectacles.*)

Professor: Eureka! I've done it! This calls for a celebration! (*He rings a bell and speaks down a tube.*) Steward! Bring me a reconstituted strawberry space shake, double quick! There's something I want to test out.

(*Lights up on the Space Singers, who are all wearing strange-looking glasses. As they sing the song, a mime takes place. The Professor puts on his X-ray specs. The steward enters, wearing a costume that displays his internal organs. The digestive system is much in evidence, with painted bacon and eggs piled up in the stomach area. The Professor reacts with nausea, and throws the glasses over his shoulder at the song's end.*)

Liver and lungs and veins so blue,
  X-ray vision,
I've invented something new,
  X-ray vision,
Spectacles that see through you,
  X-ray vision,
Gotta admit they're a lovely fit,
But put me off my tea a bit.

Bacon and eggs you had today,
  X-ray vision,
These glasses give the game away,
  X-ray vision,
I'll take them off without delay,
  X-ray vision,
Gotta admit they're a lovely fit,
But put me off my dinner a bit.

Muscles and bones and kidneys too,
  X-ray vision,
Most unpleasant things to view,
  X-ray vision,
Imagine what I'm going through,
  X-ray vision,
Gotta admit they're a lovely fit,
But put me off my friends a bit.

Space, where the planets do roll

RECORDERS, FLUTE or METALLOPHONE

F/D (Capo third fret)   B♭/G   C⁷/A⁷   F/D

Space   crew,   fly - ing   free,   Out   in   space   where   the   pla-nets   do   roll,   Tell   me

B♭/G   C⁷/A⁷   F/D   C⁷/A⁷   F/D

what   you   see   In   space, where the pla-nets do   roll.   Shoo - ting   stars,   sa - tel - lites,

Captain's voice (*in darkness*): 'Continuation of Star Captain's log. Time hangs heavily in deep space. The crew are beginning to get restless. We have been too long away from home. The Earthling is also beginning to show signs of homesickness ...'

(*Spotlight on Earthling, sitting cross-legged, looking rather lonely. The Gobbledegook steals up and places an understanding tentacle around his shoulder. Lights up on Space Singers. The Earthling can sing the first part of the verse, the crew and Space Singers sing the answering second part.*)

Space crew, flying free,
Out in space where the planets do roll,
Tell me what you see
In space, where the planets do roll.
  Shooting stars, satellites,
  Asteroids, meteorites,
  We've seen wondrous sights
  In space where the planets do roll.
  They roll and roll,
  Roll and roll,
  We've seen wondrous sights
  In space, where the planets do roll.

Space crew, dressed in blue,
Out in space where the planets do roll?
Tell me what you do
In space, where the planets do roll?
  Steer our ship, check the dials,
  Try to while away the miles,
  Dream of friendly smiles
  In space where the planets do roll.
  They roll and roll,
  Roll and roll,
  Dream of friendly smiles
  In space where the planets do roll.

36

37

Time machine

(Lights up on Professor's lab. In the middle of the floor stands the time machine. The Professor enters with the Gobbledegook and the Earthling in tow.)

Earthling: What's this, Professor?

Professor: What is it? Why, it's a time machine, of course. My latest invention. I thought you might like to be the first to try it out. This machine gives the history of all the known planets in the universe. You'll be interested in Earth, of course. You just sit inside, turn the dial to where it's marked 'Earth', and the whole of Earth's history will pass by the windows. Dinosaurs, the Stone Age, Ancient Rome, Camelot — you'll see it all as it really was. In you get. *(To the Gobbledegook)* Not you. There's only room for one.

(The Gobbledegook, spurned, buries it's head in its tentacles. The Earthling climbs in and sits before the control panel.)

Professor: Just one thing. Don't press the button marked emergency exit. Otherwise you'll be propelled into the past, which could be very dangerous. If you step out, you might influence the course of history, and we can't have that.

(The machine starts to hum. Lights up on the Space Singers. If you wish, the Space Singers could hold up paintings they have done depicting the various ages of history.)

Step up! Step up!
And visit the age of the dinosaur,
You'll hear them roar,
When you visit the past at last.

Step up! Step up!
And see for yourself how it all began
With Stone Age Man,
When you visit the past at last.

Step up! Step up!
Go back to the time of the knights of old
So brave, so bold,
When you visit the past at last.

Step up! Step up!
Pharoah and Roman and Greek and Gaul,
You'll see them all,
When you visit the past at last.

Step up! Step up!
And take your seat in the time machine,
Step up! Step up!
And you'll visit the past at last.

Step up! Step up!
And take your seat in the time machine,
Step up! Step up!
And you'll visit the past at last.

Was it a dream?

Was it a dream? Was it a dream?
Did I ride a starship through outer space?
Did I shout to the stars, let's have a race?
Did I really meet an alien with a smiling face,
Or was it a dream?

Was it a dream? Was it a dream?
Did I ride the sky like a meteor?
Did I go where no child has been before?
I think it really happened but I can't be sure,
Oh, was it a dream?

(The Earthling's voice is heard calling from the Time Machine.)

Earthling: Professor! I can see it! I can see everything! The whole of history is unfolding before my eyes!

Professor: Good, good. Turn it off, then, and out you get.

Earthling: Wait a minute. It's coming up to my own time. Look, there's my street — and there's the milkman, it must be morning. Oh, look! It's my bedroom — and there's my bed. I'm just going to pop out a moment and make sure everything's all right. I'll be right back.

Professor: No! No, remember what I told you. Don't press that button . . .

(There is a loud bang, and silence. The Professor opens the doors and looks inside. The time machine is empty.)

Professor: Too late. The Earthling's gone. It must have returned to its own space and time. Let's hope it doesn't affect the whole course of history, eh, Gobbledegook?

(The Gobbledegook shakes with sobs. The Professor sighs and gives it a comforting little pat. Lights down on lab area. Lights up on the Space Singers and on the Earthling's bedroom. The sound of bird song. Light comes through the window. The Earthling wakes, stretches, suddenly remembers. He/she runs to the window and looks out. He/she gives a sigh, then sings, with Space Singers:)

39

I built a rocket

Earthling (*speaking directly to audience*): Well? What do you think? Did the adventure really happen, or was it all a dream? One thing's for sure. I'm going to find out. I'm going to get all my friends to help me build a space ship, and I'm going back out there. If I fly high and far enough, eventually I'm sure to come across the Starship Silver Grey. I never had time to say goodbye or thank you to the Captain — and who's going to look after the Gobbledegook? (*Thrusts hands into pockets.*) And after all, I have to return these, don't I? (*Takes a pair of X-ray spectacles from pyjama pocket. Lights up on Space Singers, who sing the verses with the children, while the Earthling sings the chorus*).

Some people like to ride on a bike,
Pedalling from place to place,
Some catch a bus without any fuss,
But there ain't no buses to outer space, so
   I built a rocket, honey,
   Took all my pocket money,
   Now I'm away to Mars, for
   I want to go exploring,
   Life here can get so boring,
   I'm off to see the stars.

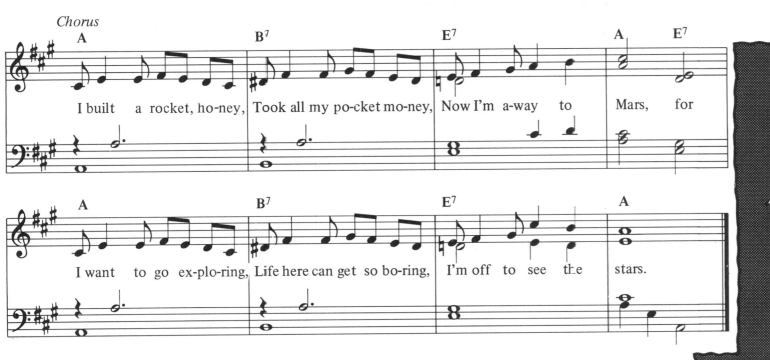

Chorus

I built a rocket, ho-ney, Took all my po-cket mo-ney, Now I'm a-way to Mars, for

I want to go ex-plo-ring, Life here can get so bo-ring, I'm off to see the stars.

Some people talk of liking to walk,
Sometimes they jog or run,
Others explain the thrill of a train
But there ain't no stations upon the sun, so
   I built a rocket, honey . . .

Some like to sail and some like to row,
Some like to fly by jet,
Planes they can fly, but not very high
And they can't quite get to the moon just yet, so
   I built a rocket, honey . . .

(chant)
**Ten – nine – eight – seven – six – five – four –
   three – two – one – BLAST OFF!**

(*During the song, a group of friends join the Earthling and make a large rocket out of junk materials. During the countdown, the rocket engines roar, the Earthling climbs in, the friends step back and in a climax of engine noise the rocket takes off, its exit screened by a smoke bomb and falling curtain. The cast take their bows.*)

A NIGHT IN SPOOKSVILLE

A comedy of music and mime

Introduction

In *A Night in Spooksville*, four lost travellers stumble upon Spooksville as night is falling, and thus begins a terrifying adventure. First the travellers encounter the Horror Hotel, where they decide not to linger. They are not tempted by the menu at the Crazy Café and blunder on into the Ghoul School. Driven away by the little ghosts' playground pranks and appalling jokes they are drawn to the weird music of the Dark Disco. They escape the clutches of their dancing partners, and hurriedly depart, singing *One night in Spooksville's quite enough for me*.

Using the material

The songs provide many opportunities for exploring sounds, mime and dance imaginatively in class, and the instrumental game *Spooksville Stroll* offers further sound exploration. For those who would like to take the material further still, a combination of the four main songs (*Horror Hotel, Crazy Café, Ghoul School* and *Dark Disco*) with *Spooksville Stroll* will provide a good half term's class work, which might be presented to the rest of the school as an informal performance. But for the really ambitious, here are some ideas for a fully staged performance

For a full performance you will need:

Narrator
Four travellers
The Spooky Duke
Ghostly waiters
Hector the Spectre, Spooky Suky, and Big Mac
Dr Phantom
Trembling Trevor
Lonely ghost and lady friend
Several dancing and miming ghosts and disco ravers
Five groups of instrumentalists to play

1. Horror Hotel link   2. Crazy Cafe link   3. Ghoul School link
4. Dark Disco link   5. Song accompaniments

The theme music you have prepared for the instrumental game, *Spooksville Stroll*, provides the link between songs, the background to the narration, and aural signposts to the lost travellers. The order of performance is:

First narration and song: **Things that go bump in the night**

Second narration and Horror Hotel link – crescendo into

The Horror Hotel

Third narration and Horror Hotel link – fade into

Three Ghosts

Fourth narration and Crazy Café link – crescendo into

Crazy Café

Fifth narration and Crazy Café link – fade into

Cold Feet

Sixth narration and Ghoul School link – crescendo into

The Ghoul School

Seventh narration and Ghoul School link – fade into

Lonely ghost

Eighth narration and Dark Disco link – crescendo into

The Dark Disco

Dark Disco link – fade into

One night in Spooksville's quite enough for me

Finale – cumulative entry of instrumental links building to huge climax of sound.

Costumes and scenery

Costumes for ghosts are easily improvised from sheets (use black felt markers for the faces). The main ghost characters will require a little more thought to distinguish them – Dr Phantom will need a stethoscope, the Ghoul School children will need satchels, and so on. Trolls and monsters are a little more tricky, but fun can be had making masks, and dressing up.

Make simple screens from paper and wooden struts showing the exteriors of the Horror Hotel and the Crazy Café, and the interiors of the Ghoul School and the Dark Disco. Light each of these areas from above with different coloured spotlights. You can mark out a street plan on the floor of the performance area in chalk or poster paint. (See page 48 for street name ideas.)

Decorate the hall with 'cobwebs' and pictures. Darken windows if you are performing during daylight, and use spotlights for the performance area. You could make a tape recording of scary sounds – doors squeaking, wind, footsteps, chains, etc – to play as the audience comes in. Make posters to advertise your musical, and programmes listing the performers and explaining the scenario.

Staging

The diagram on the next page suggests positions for a performance in the round. Ideas for mime, dance and drama are given with each song. The travellers occupy centre stage most of the time, while the rest of the cast are seated round the performance area, only entering when required.

If you can get a PA system, the narrator can be located right outside the performance area so that the audience hears only a disembodied voice.

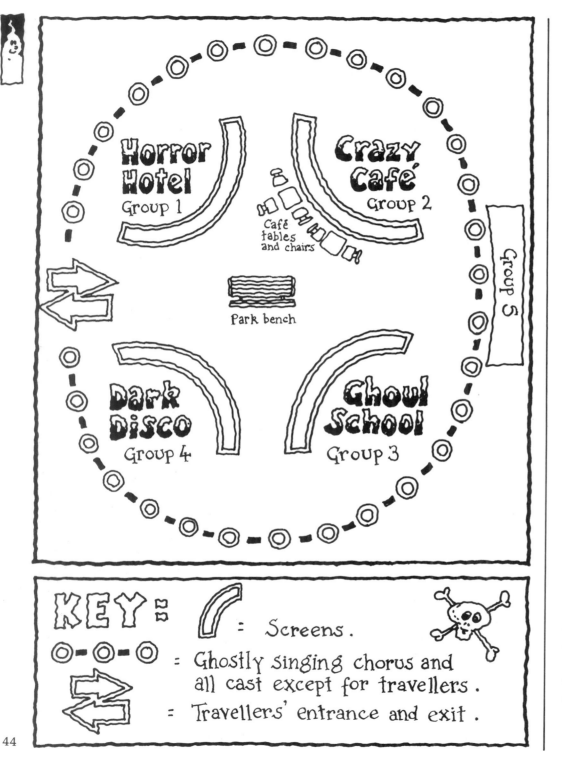

Café
tables
and chairs

Park bench

Horror
Hotel
Group 1

Crazy
Café
Group 2

Group 5

Dark
Disco
Group 4

Ghoul
School
Group 3

KEY:

⊏ = Screens.

◎-◎-◎ = Ghostly singing chorus and all cast except for travellers.

⇄ = Travellers' entrance and exit.

Spooksville stroll

The sounds you devise in this piece can be used to create a complete composition, or they can be used to link the songs in your performance of *A Night in Spooksville*.

Taking a stroll in Spooksville at night can be a dicey business. It's so dark you can't see where you are going, and you only know where you are by the sounds which jump out at you when you get there. So you know when you are in the Dark Disco because of the wild music they dance to. Standing outside the Crazy Café can be a painful experience — it's one of those places that has a small orchestra to entertain the diners (take their minds off their food, more likely). The trouble is, none of the performers actually know how to play their instruments.

Take a walk along the street to the Ghoul School and you've arrived when you hear the little ghosts practising their hollow laughter, screams, howls, shrieks, groans and squeaks. There are chains jangling, doors creaking and of course, that dreaded sound, the school bell.

The sound coming from the direction of the Horror Hotel is bloodcurdling, and it gets louder and more sinister the closer you go. It is something between the roar of a werewolf, the twitter of bats and the howl of a gale. Maniacal laughter completes the welcome.

As you move from place to place, there is the slap of your feet on the wet, cobbled streets, echoing between the walls of empty houses and the ghost-ridden alleyways of this vile little ville.

Preparation

You will need five groups of performers. Decide on how many are needed for each group after you have looked at the instrumentation and effects required.

Group 1 – Horror Hotel The strange noise coming from the Horror Hotel is made by bullroarers, with voices adding cackling, maniacal laughter. A bullroarer is a piece of wood fixed to a length of string and spun around in the air. Take a wooden ruler and make a small hole near one end. Tie a piece of string *very* firmly through the hole and whirl the ruler in a circle. As the bullroarer goes round in a large circle, it should also spin, making a whirring, buzzing, booming sound. Try out different materials and shapes – plastic container lids, carved wood – and listen to the different sounds you can produce.

Group 2 – Crazy Café The worst orchestra in the world needs violins and cellos, preferably broken and with strings missing, played by total incompetents. This group plays in waltz rhythm, with cellos playing on beat 1, and violins on beats 2 and 3. A single violin plays long held notes over the top. Substitute a bass tambour and wailing recorders if strings are not available.

Group 3 – Ghoul School Use voices and amplify them by screaming, groaning and wailing into empty buckets or metal wastepaper bins. Try howling into the soundhole of a guitar, experimenting with your voice to find the most interesting sound.

For the school bell, suspend a length of metal pipe from a piece of string and hit it with a piece of wood. Find some chains to jangle, and slowly run a fingernail along the lowest string of a guitar for the sound of a creaking door.

Group 4 – Dark Disco You will need a piano, a deep-toned drum and a wobble board. This is a large, rectangular sheet of thin plywood. Hold it out in front of you by the two shorter edges and shake it backwards and forwards. After a while you will be able to control the peculiar sound it makes and play in rhythm with the other instruments. The drum beats a relentless and steady pattern of crotchets and the piano plays random low notes, improvising around the beat.

Group 5 – the travellers Finally, moving between these strange sounds, are the travellers who all play clapper boards (see page 55). Clap the boards together at walking pace. You can practise all playing at the same time, or each in your own rhythm as though you were all walking at your own pace. (This group is not used in the full performance of *A Night in Spooksville*.)

To play you need:
A conductor
A die (a large foam one would be good)
A die thrower
6 large cards numbered 1–6 on both sides

Each group is positioned as indicated in the diagram. The travellers with their clapper boards physically move from one group to the other, starting from the middle and returning to the centre each time a 5 or 6 is thrown.

The thrower rolls the die, the conductor holds up the matching card, and the corresponding group begins to play its theme. The travellers move towards the group, playing their clapper boards until they get there. The group continues to play until a five or a six is thrown, at which the travellers return to the centre playing their clapper boards again until they arrive at another group. The piece ends when the conductor holds all the cards up at once and the groups play all together until the cards are lowered. The conductor can indicate a crescendo and decrescendo as the travellers arrive at and depart from each of the groups.

Things that go bump in the night

Narrator

When the lights go out at bedtime,
Do you turn them on again?
Do you say you've got a tummy ache
And can't sleep for the pain?
Do you howl for drinks of water
Till the grownups end up cross,
Then dive beneath the blankets
Where you shiver, shake and toss?
Do you *hate* your little brother
When he scares you for a lark?
Then the chances are, my children,
YOU ARE FRIGHTENED OF THE DARK!

**When mum turns out the electric light,
Things that go *bump*, bump in the night,
I try to be brave but I can't be, quite,
Things that go *bump*, bump in the night,
Suppose they've teeth and give me a bite,
Things that go *bump*, bump in the night,
I hope they won't but I think they might,
Things that go bump, bump in the night.**

**Mum says they're in my head,
I think they're under the bed,
Dad says they're in my mind,
I think they're right behind me,**

**Come outa there, and into the light!
Things that go *bump*, bump in the night,
Then I'll go BOO! and give you a fright,
Things that go bump in the night.
BOO!**

When mum turns out the e - lec - tric light, Things that go *bump*, bump in the night, I try to be brave but I can't be, quite, Things that go bump in the night. _____ Sup- pose they've teeth and give me a bite, Things that go *bump*, bump in the night, I hope they won't but I think they might, Things that go bump in the night.

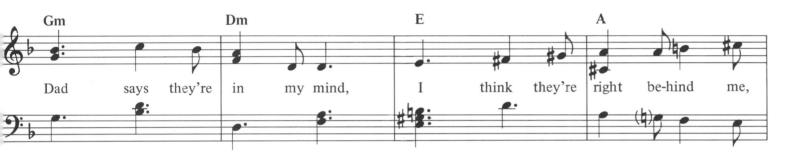

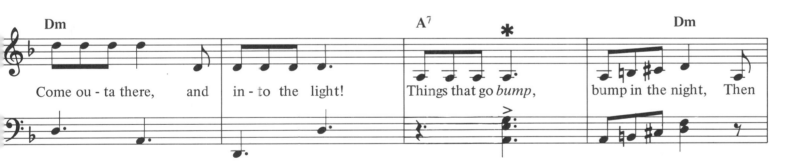

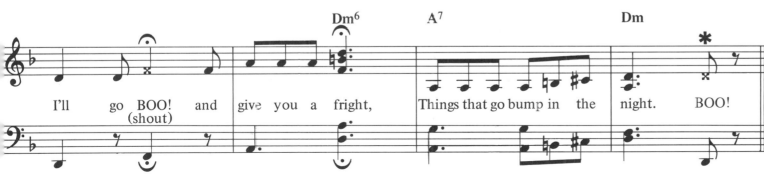

Song accompaniment

Large drum – beat loudly where you see *

Tambourine, lines 1, 3, 5, 7, 13, 15

Claves, lines 2, 4, 6, 8, 14, 16 – copy the rhythm of the melody. Singers – make big contrasts between loud and soft.

Staging

Apart from the travellers, who enter later, everyone is in position. The performance area is in semi-darkness. A small group of ghosts from the chorus converges on the centre and, as the song begins, creeps round in time to the music. In the line, 'Things that go bump, bump in the night', they jump high in the air, clap hands and shout 'bump' on the first bump. When the singers shout 'BOO!' a white spotlight can snap onto the dancers, who quickly fade back into the darkness of the chorus.

Horror Hotel

Narrator

The von Oddelot family had a gallery full of portraits of their ancestors. It was no accident that the painting of the Old Duke hung facing the wall. His brother put it that way.

The Old Duke's name was Nastius. Duke Nastius von Oddelot. Nobody in the family mentioned his name. They were all too ashamed of the *terrible things* he did. Like talking with his mouth full, running off with the valuable family collection of scented egg cosies, biting the dog, playing the trumpet at night. Things like that. Why, even when he was ninety-seven years old, they caught him trying to drown the goldfish!

On the night of his hundredth birthday, he vanished. Nobody knows what became of him, but rumour has it that his ghost is up to no good somewhere – probably running a hotel in Spooksville.

Turn right down Sinister Street
Then cut through Panicky Park,
Turn left at Cold Feet Lane,
Where it's always dim and dark,
Head then for Horror Hotel
Arising from the gloom,
You can be sure that you won't sleep well
But you'll always get a room, for
   The Spooky Duke runs this town's hotel,
   What a laugh, it's an empty shell,
   The roof's long gone and the walls as well,
   And your host's a ghost!

Some stay at the Holiday Inn
Some rent out a penthouse suite,
Few dwell in Horror Hotel
Where the waiter wears a sheet,
Pull hard on the big brass bell,
You will always get a bed,
You can be sure that you won't sleep well
And could end up dead instead, for
   The Spooky Duke runs this town's hotel . . .

Hor-ror Ho - tel A - ris - ing from the gloom,

You can be sure that you won't sleep well But you'll

rall.

al - ways get a room, for *Chorus* The Spooky Duke runs this town's ho - tel,

What a laugh, it's an

emp - ty shell, The roof's long gone and the walls as well, And your host's a ghost!

Staging

First verse – the travellers enter (they are cheerful and unsuspecting). They approach the hotel, indicating to each other that they could sleep there.

Chorus – hollow laughter from the hotel makes the travellers draw back fearfully.

Second verse – they approach again and bravely mime pulling the door bell. The Spooky Duke opens the door and the travellers flee to centre stage.

Chorus – the Spooky Duke capers around in front of the hotel before retreating back inside as the song closes.

Song accompaniment

The introduction can be played very softly as an interlude during which you might add some of these sound effects. Guitars are very good for creaks and squeaks and patterings. Party balloons make excruciating noises when rubbed with the hands. Make a tube rattle for very quiet pattering sounds. Tip it so that the lentils patter down from one end to the other:

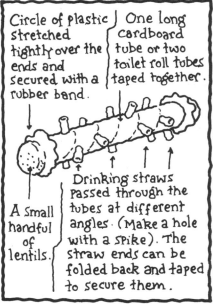

Circle of plastic stretched tightly over the ends and secured with a rubber band.

One long cardboard tube or two toilet roll tubes taped together.

A small handful of lentils.

Drinking straws passed through the tubes at different angles. (Make a hole with a spike). The straw ends can be folded back and taped to secure them.

Verse and chorus

Drum (tap lightly – hard stick)

Guiro

Claves or clappers

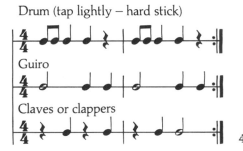

49

Three ghosts

Narrator

Just like human beings, ghosts vary. Some walk around with their heads tucked beneath their arms, wearing ruffled collars and thick tights to keep the draughts out. Some clank around in suits of armour — they are usually the noisiest of the lot. Others prefer to shuffle about with chains wrapped around their feet, moaning because their ankles are sore. Others you can hardly see at all, you just feel a bit chilly when they pass by. The places ghosts choose to haunt vary too. Not all of them go for the obvious, such as ruined castles and empty houses. Take Big Mac, for example. He likes to haunt supermarkets, because he loves eating, and can stuff himself with ice cream from the freezer all night long. And have you heard of Spooky Suky, who is so small she haunts telephone boxes? Or Hector the Spectre who is so big he has trouble finding a place vast enough to hold him? Ghosts vary. Just like people.

I'm Hector the Spectre the HUGE ghost
As everyone ought to know,
And I'm gonna haunt a cathedral
'Cos I need the space to grow.
    Hector the Spectre the HUGE ghost . . . (whisper)

I'm Spooky Suky the small ghost,
You'll find me near the ground,
And I'm gonna haunt this phone box,
It's the smallest place I've found.
    Spooky Suky the small ghost . . . (whisper)

I'm Big Mac the GREEDY ghost,
I wear a king-size sheet,
And I'm gonna haunt in Safeway's
'Cos I like a lot to eat.
    Big Mac the GREEDY ghost . . . (whisper)

    WHICH GHOST DO YOU
    LIKE THE MOST? *(shout)*

Singing the song

Divide the ghost chorus into three groups. Group 1 sings the first verse, then whispers 'Hector the Spectre the huge ghost', and continues to whisper it as Group 2 sings the second verse. Group 1 and 2 continue whispering their lines while Group 3 sings the last verse. The last line is shouted in unison.

Song accompaniment

Think of sound effects to accompany each ghost's verse, e.g. a bass xylophone tolling the note D for Hector the Spectre, finger cymbals for Spooky Suky, bass piano chords or clusters for Big Mac.

Staging

Travellers – huddle centre stage.

Three ghosts – verses: each ghost in turn comes forward from the chorus ring and circles the travellers.

Whispered chorus – actions. Hector the Spectre crouches, grows and stretches high on 'huge', Spooky Suky does the opposite, and Big Mac spreads his sheet out wide.

Whoooo are yoooou?
(game)

Everybody draws a picture of a ghostly character. Then the class splits up into pairs. One person in each pair imagines that they are the character they have drawn and the other person interviews them, asking what they do with their time, what their likes and dislikes are, when they were born, where they live, when they died, etc. The person giving the interview should try to build up a convincing picture of the character by trying to think what it is really like to be that ghost. Change over.

Crazy Café

Narrator

Most people believe that ghosts live on a diet of fresh air. Nothing could be further from the truth. Ghosts, just like anyone else, like regular meals. Phantom splodge, spookhetti, ghoulash and scream cakes are just some of the most popular ghostly dishes.

What's on the menu at Crazy Café?
  Crazy Café, Crazy Café,
What's on the menu at Crazy Café?
  What's on the menu today?

We've got Trouser Sandwich, Scrambled Sock,
Hard-boiled Bugs and Roasted Clock,
Glass Soup and Jellyfish Jam,
And Fillet of Ferret is the special, madame.
  What's on the menu at Crazy Café ...

We've got Toasted Matchbox, Grated Cork,
Hot Cross Grandad, Curried Fork,
Glass Soup and Jellyfish Jam,
And Fillet of Ferret is the special, madame.

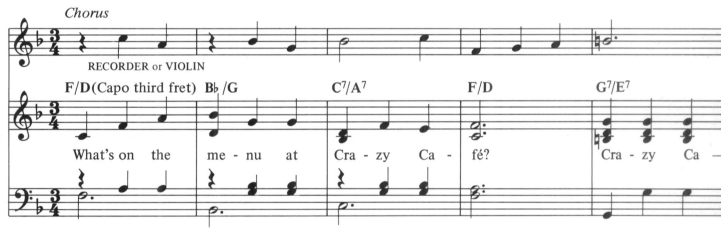

Verse

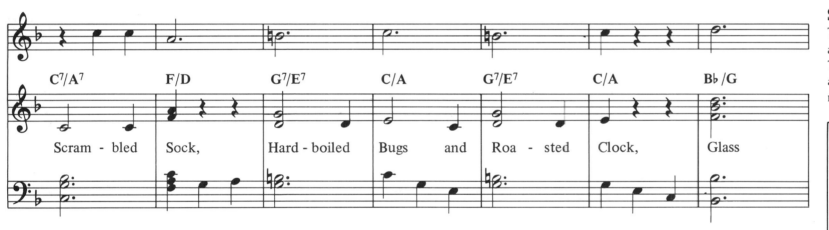

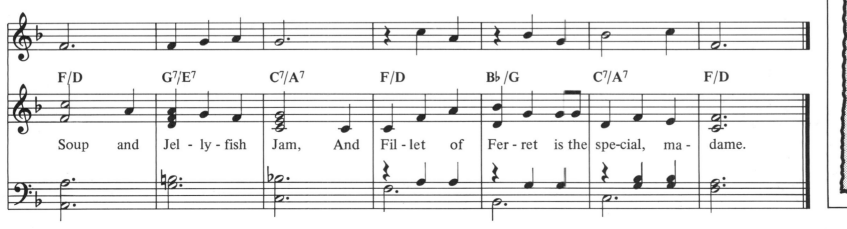

Song accompaniment

Make up an accompaniment using the waltz rhythm of the song – a heavy beat followed by two light beats:

Slap a table top or hard surface with your hand on the first beat, and jangle a bag of cutlery on the second and third beats.

Try making up some crazy sound effects to play when each item on the menu is sung.

Staging

The travellers approach and sit down at the tables outside the Crazy Cafe. They sing the chorus. Ghostly waiters appear and sing the verses, displaying menus.

Crazy anagrams

The cook at the Crazy Café is worse at spelling than he is at cooking. What do you think these dishes are?

Crazy Café
menu

RACE MICE . . . .
SAD AL . . . .
LONE DAME . . . .
CRUFTI NOSES . . . . . .
SPICE AND CHIP . . . . .
FOOT TAPE . . . .
TED BED AN' RAT BRU . . .
NEW SAC DISH . . . .

53

Cold feet

Narrator

Not many people realise this, but ghosts sometimes have problems with their health. Dr Phantom, Spooksville's general practitioner, has come across many strange cases in his time – but none quite so perplexing as that of Trembling Trevor. Trevor suffered from a whole host of ailments, including butterflies in his tummy, gooseflesh, collywobbles, heebie-jeebies and above all, cold feet. In other words, he was scared. He hated going out haunting, especially when it was dark, and all the other ghosts teased him something rotten. Dr Phantom tried everything to cure poor Trevor. He gave him an anti heebie-jeebie injection, but that just made the collywobbles worse. The butterflies in Trevor's tummy just played ping pong with the pills he swallowed. The gooseflesh remained however much ointment he rubbed in. Finally, exasperated, Dr Phantom had to resort to several pairs of woolly socks. He wasn't really into alternative medicine, but he had to admit they worked!

Doctor Phantom, what can I do?
No one knows, so I'm asking you,
Here's the problem, short and sweet,
I got – cold feet!
   Cold, feet, cold feet,
   Shiver-his-frozen-toesy,
   But he's got cold feet!
   Cold feet!

All the ghosts look down on me,
I don't get no sympathy,
I don't want to walk the street
With my – cold feet!
   Cold feet, cold feet . . .

Other ghosts go out to moan,
I prefer to stay at home,
I don't like to leave the heat
With my – cold feet!
   Cold feet, cold feet . . .

Song accompaniment

Clapper boards — to make some large clapper boards, which sound like the slap of cold feet on wet streets, cut two pieces of hardboard 12×20 cm. Tie on string handles by making holes near the ends of the boards, pushing the string through and knotting it (see diagram). The string should be just long enough to push your hand between it and the board. Hold one board in each hand and slap them against each other crossways so that the ends of string do not get between the boards. Try slapping in this rhythm:

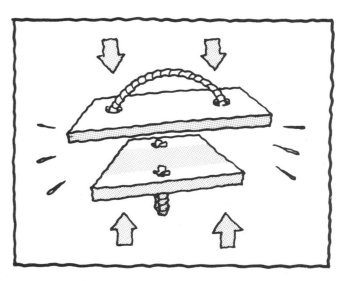

Singing the song

Trevor sings the verses. The ghost chorus sings the chorus.

Staging

Travellers retreat to centre stage again. Dr Phantom and Trembling Trevor enter and carry one of the Crazy Café tables and two chairs into an open space. Trembling Trevor indicates his cold feet (painted blue?), and Dr Phantom produces potions and finally socks from under his sheet.

Ghoul School

Narrator

As the notes of the evening hymn die away, the Head floats up to the platform and stares down at the assembled phantoms who sit cross-legged on the floor. Those who have no legs cross their eyes and hope for the best.

'Now then,' says the Head. 'We have some new pupils starting Ghoul School tonight. Stand up, you new little ones.'

Three small ghosts drift to their feet, looking shy.

'Nothing to be scared of,' says the Head kindly. 'It's all very easy. Chain rattling's first on the timetable, followed by creaking, shrieking, squeaking, sneaking, peeking, and speaking-in-deep-scary-voices. Then we have dinner. Tonight there is ghoulash with a choice of screech melba or dread-and-flutter-pudding.'

'Hooray!' wail the ghosts.

'And tonight, everyone must be on their best behaviour. The Chief Spectre is paying a visit, so keep your sheets clean and don't wail unless you're wailed to. That will be all. Dismiss.'

The Head floats off to join its body, which is busily writing notes to parents in the office, while the little ghouls run out to play.

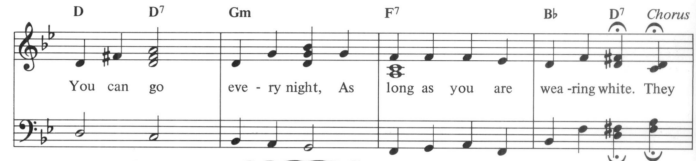

Don't despair, don't feel blue,
If you're a ghost, there's a school for you.
You can go every night,
As long as you are wearing white.
 They don't teach writing at the Ghoul School,
 They just teach frighting at the
  Ghoul School,
 You'll learn how to moan and groan
 At the School for Ghouls.
 They don't teach spelling at the
  Ghoul School,
 They just teach yelling at the Ghoul School,
 You'll learn how to sigh and cry
 At the School for Ghouls.

Meet the Head, Mr Cross,
He's got no body but he's still the boss,
The phantom staff are there to teach,
You'll learn to weep and wail and screech,
 They don't teach writing at the
  Ghoul School . . .

don't teach wri-ting at the Ghoul School, They just teach frigh-ting at the Ghoul School, You'll

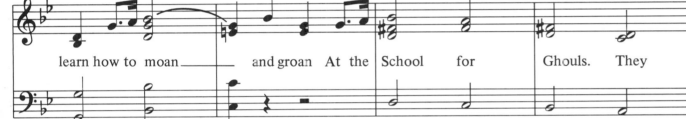

learn how to moan ___ and groan At the School for Ghouls. They

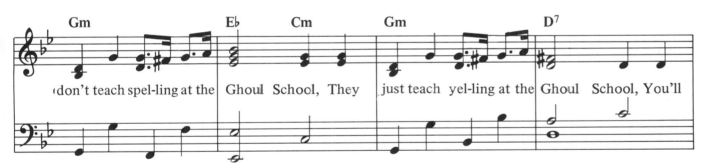

(don't teach spel-ling at the Ghoul School, They just teach yel-ling at the Ghoul School, You'll

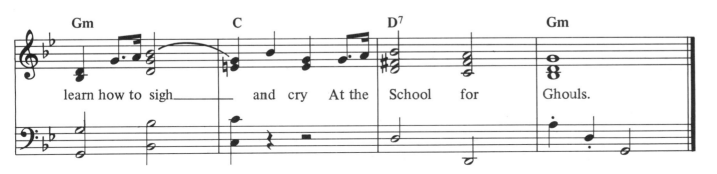

learn how to sigh ___ and cry At the School for Ghouls.

Song accompaniments

Chorus – choose two small groups, one to moan, the other to sigh.

sigh   moan

Verse – percussion

Clapping/claves

Guiro

Indian bells

Staging

Groups of little ghouls enter and sit down in rows. The travellers approach and sit in the back row. The Head's voice is played by the narrator, while the Head himself can have a black cloak covering him from the neck down. During the song the little phantoms draw the travellers into their ring games and jokes. At the end they file off to their seats, leaving the travellers reeling and bewildered.

Ghoul School Jokes

57

Lonely ghost

Narrator

Gary the ghost was feeling sorry for himself. He was bored and lonely – even walking through walls and wailing had lost their charm. Very few people noticed him these days. He seemed to be getting fainter somehow. On the rare occasions when someone *did* spot him, they just said, 'Oh, hello Garry, almost didn't see you,' and passed on.

His chains were getting rusty and losing their clank. His sheet was full of moth holes. What was the point of taking a pride in his appearance when, as far as most people were concerned, he didn't even *appear?* What he needed most of all was a companion – someone who would be his friend, perhaps even a *girlfriend*! It was time for action. What he decided to do was this. He would compose a sad poem and send it to the Lonely Hearts column of the local paper. Perhaps a girl ghost would see it and want to be his friend. He found some paper and a pencil, and worked on the poem for days. After several attempts he had something which went like this:

It's a lonely life, a ghost's life,
But nobody seems to care,
Nobody stops to have a chat
'Cos nobody knows you're there.
You wail a bit, or walk through a wall,
Or sit and rattle your chain,
But things like that can fall a bit flat
When you do them again and again.
Perhaps it's time I got married,
I'd give her a bunch of flowers,
We'd walk the streets in clean, white sheets
And rattle our chains for hours.

Said the ghost to the lady, will you have this dance,
  have this dance, have this dance?
But she passed on by without a single glance,
So he never stood the ghost of a chance.
  Poor ghost, lonely ghost,
  No one understands your plight,
  Poor ghost, lonely ghost,
  You wail all day and you moan all night.
  Ooooooooooo! Ooooooooooo!

Said the ghost to the children, won't you come and play,
  come and play, come and play?
But they couldn't see him and they ran away,
So he cried in a corner all day.
  Poor ghost, lonely ghost...

Then the ghost met another with a smile so sweet,
  smile so sweet, smile so sweet,
Each got married in a clean, white sheet,
And now this little story's complete.
  Poor ghost, lonely ghost...

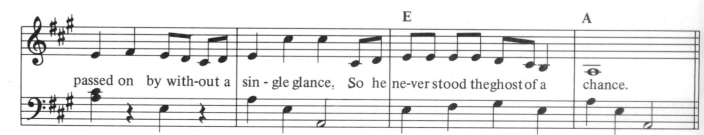

Song accompaniment

Triangle – first beat of each bar in the verse.

Violins – pluck the notes marked above the stave.

Chime bars, bars 17–20 (Ooooooooooo)

Tambourine, bars 17–20

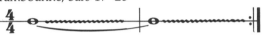

Staging

A despondent Gary enters and flops into a chair outside the Crazy Café. He takes out paper and pen and writes.

First verse – mimes inviting café waitress to dance.

Chorus – walks away from table wringing hands and sobbing.

Second verse – small group of Ghoul School children pass him by.

Chorus – as before.

Third verse – sits at bench, head between hands, throws poem on floor. Glamorous ghost picks it up, reads it, and introduces herself. They dance off hand in hand.

Dark Disco

Narrator

The Dark Disco is held every Saturday night. It's a popular event with the local ghostly residents, of course — but it also attracts a very mixed crowd from far and wide. The sort of types who wouldn't be welcome anywhere else, mainly because of their bad reputation and even worse dress sense. The word has got round that at the Dark Disco in Spooksville, anything goes — therefore it's always packed out with undesirables. Skeletons, witches, trolls, goblins, bogeymen, vampires — you name it, every Saturday night they all pile in, determined to enjoy themselves. Some arrive on broomsticks, some in black coaches pulled by plumed horses, some in hired buses, some on bicycles. The streets are packed with visitors, and the queue outside the Dark Disco stretches round the town.

You'd never think they'd all fit in — but somehow, they do, and spend a happy night capering away to the latest sounds — *The Funky Yeti*, *Dracula Rap*, *Bogeyman Boogie* — and, of course, the highly popular smash hit, *Ghouls Were Made To Love And Kiss*.

As the first rays of the sun touch the horizon, everyone leaves, tired but happy — and stroll home arm in arm, bellowing a last chorus of *You'll Never Squawk Alone*, by *The Screaming Banshees*.

It really is a great night out. You should see the holes in the floor.

If you're not too scared to take the chance,
Saturday night, it's the Monsters' Dance —
   Take the risk and go,
   Take the risk and go,
   Take the risk and go to the Dark Disco,
   Where the bogey-men boogie on a Saturday night.

Well the giants do the jive, the trolls try to sing,
The Loch Ness Monster does the Highland Fling —
   Take the risk and go . . .

The witches do the waltz, the spooks start to spin,
The yetis start a-poppin' and the floor caves in —
   Take the risk and go . . .

The zombie likes to jig, the werewolf likes to rap,
The wizard and the warlock like to clap, clap, clap —
   Take the risk and go . . .

The DJ is Dracula. Ooh! that smile!
His teeth are spectacular, he cleans them with a file —
   Take the risk and go . . .

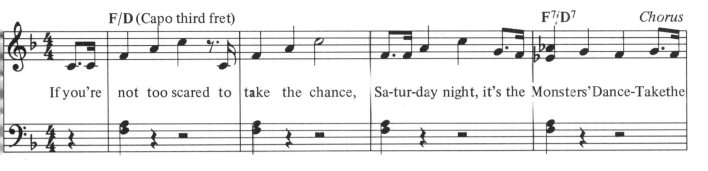

F/D (Capo third fret)   F⁷/D⁷   *Chorus*

If you're not too scared to take the chance, Sa-tur-day night, it's the Monsters' Dance—Take the

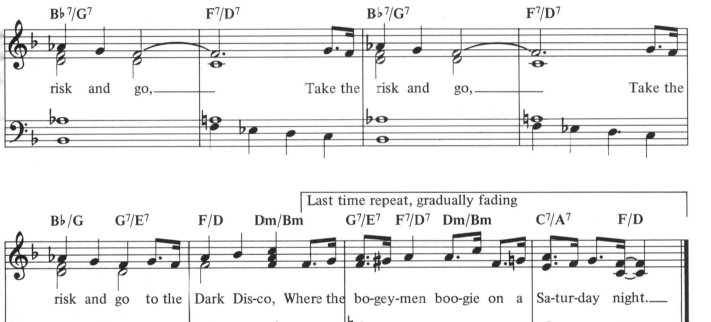

Bb⁷/G⁷   F⁷/D⁷   Bb⁷/G⁷   F⁷/D⁷

risk and go,_____ Take the risk and go,_____ Take the

Last time repeat, gradually fading

Bb/G   G⁷/E⁷   F/D   Dm/Bm   G⁷/E⁷   F⁷/D⁷   Dm/Bm   C⁷/A⁷   F/D

risk and go to the Dark Dis-co, Where the bo-gey-men boo-gie on a Sa-tur-day night.___

Song accompaniment

Snare drum with wire brush – improvise around this rhythm:

Body percussion – try clapping on the off beat first:

Then make up some more elaborate patterns, e.g.

Snap fingers

Slap knees

Stamp feet

Clap

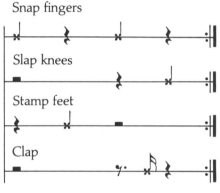

Staging

Narration – the revellers stream into town and queue up outside the disco.

Song – invent dances for each of the characters, so that during the verses each can invite a traveller to partner him. Fill the floor with twisting, gyrating dancers. In the last verse, the travellers break away from their partners and huddle in the centre. After the song the revellers disperse as the link music fades away.

Make up a top ten list of the records that get played at the Dark Disco, and name the groups that made them e.g.

Breakin' with the broomstick – Wicked Wanda and the Cool Cats.

61

One night in Spooksville's quite enough for me

One night in Spooksville's quite enough for me, for me,
One night in Spooksville's quite enough for me,
I've had more than enough of wails and moaning,
More than enough of squeaks and groaning,
One night in Spooksville's quite enough,
One night in Spooksville's quite enough for me.

One night in Spooksville's quite enough for me, for me,
One night in Spooksville's quite enough for me,
I've had more than enough of all things eerie,
I'm going home 'cos I feel weary,
One night in Spooksville's quite enough,
One night in Spooksville's quite enough for me.

Staging

The travellers sing as they make their way back to the place where they came in, and exit still singing.

Singing the song

The travellers take a solo line each, singing the middle section together.

As the travellers' song fades with them into the distance, the hotel band starts its theme very quietly, and is joined in turn by each of the other three bands. They crescendo together up to a final cymbal clash as the lights come on. Travellers and ghosts return hand in hand to take their bow.

Index of first lines

First published 1988 by A & C Black (Publishers) Ltd
35 Bedford Row, London WC1R 4JH
Text and music © 1988 Kaye Umansky
Illustrations © 1988 Chris Smedley

ISBN 0–7136–3072–8

Music set by Linda Lancaster
Designed by Janet Watson
Printed in Great Britain by Hollen Street Press Limited
Slough, Berkshire